Helena & Daedo

(Part 1)

A Hot & Steamy Aurelia Hilton's Romance Short Novel Book 29

By Aurelia Hilton

Table of Contents

Chapter 1

The morning sunlight came out as the nation of Leno awoke to another day. Since they had endured a full month of snow, the warmth was going to be a welcome break. Leno was a rich island in the Mediterranean Sea. Yet, from the time it was first occupied, Leno had severed all ties with the rest of the world, and as a result, it became a closed off country.

Although her citizens could travel away, no one from the outside world would be granted permanent residency in Leno. The country was ruled by a royal family, so when a monarch passed away, the eldest in the family would ascend the throne. Their economy was not like any other in the world. They had no banking system and money was obsolete. The Lenos only heard of how people elsewhere in distant lands worked so hard in order to get paid, and how some of them were worth a lot whereas others had nothing. It wasn't as if Leno hadn't ever been witness to misery; it was there, except it seldom came around. Although Leno had abolished money from their economy, their social structure was terribly discriminative, for people were born into either nobility, middle society, or the low class. The men born into high society automatically held authority, those at the middle usually took up roles in organized sectors like education, and the low class was assigned to manual work. But they also lived in poorly maintained shelters. The country had three official Cantons; Katol, which was home to aristocrats; Lepan, home to the average people; and Thirta, an isolated region bordering on the shore, where the low class settled. Basic education was compulsory, which had also been stratified, in order to stop people from mixing. The only way a low class could ascend into high society was in the rare incident of marrying up.

In the poor district of Thirta, there lived a woman named Helena, she was the eldest in her family, and her mother was desperate to give her away to a man. Helena was a tall woman with stern eyes and a bold walking style. When she walked in the road, the men would whistle at her, but she never turned at them, so the men believed she was proud. Obviously, she was in need of a husband, but she'd only listen to men who came up to her and said what they wanted. There was a man named Micah in their residence who worked in a garage. Micah had tried so hard to win her heart but she could tell he was a fake. Maybe if he'd stayed at a distance to make her feel ignored, he might have got a chance, but Micah was as pushy as can be, always popping out of nowhere, grinning and asking the same questions over and over again.

"Exc'se me, Helena, is your papa back from the sea yet?" It looked like concern at first. But slowly she realized that Micah might be looking to inflame her father so he'd wife her on his word!! That was a terrible thought, but it was still there, and now she'd escalate her indifference into open hostility.

"Is your papa back yet, Helena?" "Get the hell out of here, Micah, you swine!"

Helena's father had worked at the sea since his youth. He had been a cook in a ship for 30 years and had now reached the age at which he must stop working. So he knew too well that when they docked at the shores of Leno he'd be out of a job and that would be in a few months.

Whenever her dad was at home she'd be in high spirits. Sadly, she never had a special bond with her mother, and because of that, she felt terrible. Well, her mother couldn't care less, for she had twin boys that she adored. Helena thought that maybe when she'd get married she'd for once make her mother happy. So, she purposed to get herself a man; any other man except the dangerous Micah.

The twins shrieked as they ran out of the house; Luka was running after Jako, while holding up a stick, meaning to smack him. A second later Helena's mother stood at the door and yelled, "Stop that game before I bash your heads!" Suddenly the boys slowed down and grinned as they walked across the compound, with Jako warily glancing back at Luka. It was Saturday morning. They only day the entire nation would skip work and go for prayers. Helena could smell her mother's perfume as she'd prepared herself already. Furtively, she looked at the door, at her mother, and slowly walked up to her.

"Momma, I want to talk with you."

"Ah, Helena, you've not dressed up yet?"

She looked down, and then looked away, and turned around to leave. But her mother held her shoulder and asked, "What's the matter?"

"The telephone line...could you please ask the chief to replace it?"

Her mother laughed and said, "Ah, I knew it! You wanted to complain! Helena, you irritate me! You could follow on the repair yourself! Or you think you're still a small girl?"

"Momma!" Helena said and looked in her eyes. "I don't have an Identity card. How will the chief locate our house?"

She gave Helena a stern look, then turned away and walked back in the house. Helena glanced about the compound and she spotted Luka and Jako standing in a quiet corner, looking at her. She beckoned to them and they came running, crashing into her thighs. They were fraternal twins and Helena really liked them. The school was altering these two fellows a lot, though. Now they seemed to do curious deeds, speak in an odd tongue, smile at girls, and a lot of things about them were starting to not look innocent anymore. But she was still their big sister and she wanted the best for them. She liked Jako, especially when he'd smile and snug in her arms.

"The two of you - go and get dressed!" She said after lacking anything else meaningful to tell them.

"Why doesn't momma like you?" It was Luka, and quickly Helena curled her mouth, and said, "Of course she likes me. We just don't seem to agree on a lot."

"Luka, let's go and get dressed." Jako said and tugged at his brother's shoulder while giving Helena that look. Helena stood at the door and realized how she missed her dad. If she'd get a technician to repair the phone then she'd be able to call her dad. She thought on all methods possible and saw that only her Momma could save the situation. Frowning, she let off the thought. Then Helena went back to her room and changed into a dress, skipping a bath. It was a law that everyone must attend prayers in the town hall on Saturday. In each canton, the King had been represented by a team of noblemen who wore robes and stood on a platform to teach about honoring God. Although families normally went there as a unit, Helena always stayed behind to let her Momma and the twins go first, but she'd come later on, and after prayers, they'd go back as one. Obviously, it was so agonizing to be unaccepted by your mother, although she tried to not let it bother her much. In a lot of families, Saturday marked the day when they'd get together, sit down to a wonderful meal, and have fun. It was like that in Helena's home too, although she'd go away after the meal, too afraid that her Momma would tackle her. Whenever Helena prayed to God she only asked for a decent man to marry her. For that was her only chance to ever look pleasant for her mother. Helena loathed Saturdays, for they brought tears.

Helena is now 20 years old; the age at which offspring of the low class begun to till public land, and at this age one was given an identity card. The ID"s were used for effective administration, as well as to track down a person's home; which was done frequently, as every other day people were arrested and sent away to the King's court to face trials. In this Kingdom, there was only one type of people who lived in peace; the law abiders.

On Sunday morning, Helena woke up, took a bath, and put on her coveralls. If she got late for work she'd be punished. Quickly, she walked out of their house and marched to the train station. There were many others like her waiting at the station. A short time later, a two-wagon train burned down the rails and came to a stop. It had only one entrance. The doors were parted open, and immediately the men started to push and jostle, so as to get the back seats. Helena too got into the mob and she was almost crushed. Quickly, she tried to step back, but calloused hands stroked her bottom. She let out a yell and wrestled out of the crowd. Then she saw the women had wisely waited for the men to get in first, so they'd climb in last and occupy the empty front seats. On that first ride to the barley farm, Helena had thought that that behavior as childish, and then she remembered her incident and actually laughed. The train was going at a mild pace, and they'd travel for like three hours more, to arrive at their assigned barley farm. A young woman was seated next to her, leaning her head on the window, her eyes shut. But most of the men were making noise in the back. Helena thought of her circumstances and just lifted her eyebrows, weighed down. This was their system. Her mistake was to be born in the wrong society.

Leno had a localized design, where analogous places were clustered together like farms were terribly large fields. But there were many picking points across the canton and the work was divided in respect to age. Time wore on, and Helena saw in the distance a rice field stretching out. There were yellow tractors abandoned on the farm. And point shadows of men could be seen plod through the muck. Their train was headed for another farm, so they sped along the rails, as Helena looked out at the boundless stretches of fields.

Finally, the train slowed down, and the rims screeched a little until it stopped. Looking out, Helena saw a crowd of men with horses, wearing matching uniform and gaiters, and they had pistols at their waists. When the train stopped, some of the men cantered at the station and dismounted. The horses neighed and picked up their legs. Helena thought, wow. She tried to lean her head out and look carefully but was unable to see further. The train was still silent and Helena felt as if she might stand up and be the first to walk out. Suddenly, a man with an enormous face climbed in, almost tripping at the entrance. His head was clean shaven and his scraggly chin looked like a patch of small thorns.

"Good morning."

"Good morning, sir." The trainload responded nearly lethargically, and the man thundered, "I can't hear you!!"

"Good morning, sir!"

He took his time to stare at the passengers with an odd smile as if sizing them up. Helena could tell he was a man that liked to see people trembling in front of him. *Oh God*, she thought, *this is not good*. The man opened his mouth to speak and Helena noted his teeth were tiny and discolored. He was saying, "I understand that most of you are reporting for the first day. So now you're officially adults." He paused, in the tradition of public speakers, as if he was giving a commencement speech. "Adulthood comes with responsibility." He scratched his beard aggressively with another stupid smile. "How many of you have ID"s? Show me your hands." He counted a few hands in the back. "If I've counted your hand please step out." The nine men quietly walked down the aisle and stepped out and the man followed them. A few minutes later, he walked back in, looking fierce. Then another man came in, a thin man, holding a large box, and stood near him, and looked out at us aggressively.

"I'm going to give you a tag each. It has your registration number." The large man said, and Helena thought he sounded uninspiring. "So, let's start with this side, get up quickly." The women nervously got up and walked to the door, and as each of them stepped out, an oval Velcro pad was stuck in their chest. A number was printed out in the pad. Outside, in a tent, one wrote down their number, and their name, and their parents, and then their photo was taken. The government had a record of all its citizens, so they'd first check on their files before printing out IDs. It felt as if one was a prisoner but that wasn't the hardest part.

The crowd increased as people listed their identities. An enormous truck appeared in the distance, barreling down the road leaving a trail of dust. It stopped a short distance away from the crowd. Although people had started to warm up to each other with idle talk, Helena isolated herself, to quietly look at the fields. She had a lot of questions on her mind but she thought that this was just not the right time to ask.

"Hey, make ten straight lines!" A voice shouted, interrupting Helena's train of thoughts, and she turned around. Goodness, it was a soldier! They formed the queues hastily. The soldier ordered ten men to follow him to the back of the truck, and the men came back lugging crates of food. Each person was given a lunch box, and walked up to the back of the truck to pick up a hoe, and then went to the field for more instructions. The food was manioc and fillet which filled up Helena's stomach. At the field, work was done in horizontal rows, which advanced up to a border. And then they'd move to the next task. It was back-breaking work. To make matters worse, soldiers riding horses kept guard on the farmers, ordering them back to work after short breaks, and stopping fights between workers, and quelling aggression. The workers took an instant dislike to the soldiers. In the other fields seen from afar, veteran workers were there, but their routine was pretty much the same.

In a few weeks, Helena had merged into the system and became effective. The work was wearisome, so her hands got calloused. She seemed to forget about her worries pretty fast now that she was held in some activity.

But then a day came that turned her world upside down. It began very well and they divided themselves up in groups of eight each. In her group, Helena was the only female. They had been posted to dig a tunnel along the border of the field. All was well until a soldier came on his horse, making his round, checking and seeing that all was fine. Then he turned around and started to move away. Suddenly, a man stood at the tunnel and hurled a big stone at the soldier. But it missed him and instead crashed into the horse's neck, so she neighed in anguish, picking up her legs. Wrathfully, the soldier jumped off and drew his gun and aimed at the man. "Who did that?"

"It wasn't me I swear!" The man said, and instantly a blast went off; the man saw blood running down his leg; God, he'd been shot! "I'll ask you one more time; who flung that stone?"

The man broke into tears; "it's her!" he said and pointed at the shocked Helena.

"Of course it's not me! It was him!" Helena said, angrily.

"Who was it? Was it her?" The soldier asked the other men, looking at each one of them and receiving a nod that it was her. "Come here, woman."

Tears rolled out of her eyes, "These men are lying." Then she looked at them, "Why are you doing these to me? It was that man I swear!"

"I said come here!" The soldier yelled and went at her, grabbed her arm, and pulled her out. She quaked and began sobbing. The soldier dragged her toward the horse and lifted her onto the horse. Then he mounted behind her and pulled on the reins. They set off at a canter. There was a station at the gate which served as the administrative center. A few of the soldiers were drinking beer just outside. They came up and stopped in front of the office. The soldier got off and pulled down Helena. She squeaked in terror, as the soldier held her by the hair and dragged her into the office.

"What's the matter, Sergeant?" A large soldier seated behind the desk asked while looking at Helena as if she was a little piece of shit. The man had a dark monocle covering his right eye and Helena was terrified of him. She took quick short breaths, fighting back tears unsuccessfully.

"Tell the general what you have done." The soldier said and released her hair and folded his arms. She turned her soft eyes at him, "Those men lied to you, and it wasn't me!"

"Sir, the lady smacked your horse." The soldier reported, satisfied with himself.

"Go back to work and leave her with me."

"I'm innocent," Helena said when the soldier gave her a final look, before turning away to leave. Now her whole body started to vibrate with terror. It seemed like the general was in the middle of looking at the papers and having a cup of tea. After a moment of staring at the paper, the general rose up and walked in front, locked the door, and then walked behind his desk. He was so enormous and his trousers seemed wedged up between his thighs.

"Why would you hit my horse?" The general asked in a croaky voice.

The question jumbled Helena's thoughts, confusing her. "We were digging...then the soldier came...and his horse was hit...no, a man threw a stone at the soldier...but he ducked and the stone struck the horse instead...but I know the man who did that. If you let me, I can take to you to him."

A long time passed without the general saying anything, which scared Helena to her bone. Finally, he said, "What's your name?"

Trembling, she said, "I'm Helena."

"Helena, listen up if I ask you another question I simply want an answer, is that alright?"

"Yes, sir."

"No one ever hurt the King's babies and walked away scot-free. If you'd hit the soldier instead, I'd punish you and send you back to work, but hurting one of the King's babies on purpose? You have no option but to pay for it. Helena, hand me your ID."

Softly, she said, "I don't have one, for I'm recently twenty, but please let it pass."

"You're twenty, but old enough to face the law." The general retorted, picking up a phone handle and dialing a number. The line went through. He cleared his throat and said, "Lieutenant, I've got another case; crime on an animal; the accused is with me, ask your men to hurry." Then for a time he listened, and replied, "No, it's a she." And finally, he said, "Thanks." The general looked at Helena, who had dropped her head, rubbing her thumb on her palm. "Go into that room and wait there!" He roared, and Helena was startled, "I beg your pardon, sir!" "I said get the hell out of my office!" Miraculously, she remembered what he'd ordered first. Hastily, she looked for the door to the other room, walked up and opened it, and then she got in and shut the door after her, breaking into tears. Then there was a sharp movement. Helena looked up and saw a man lying on the floor, his shirt was red from blood, and the eyes had swelled out and turned blue-black with blows.

"Lady, please fetch me that glass!" The man groaned, pointing at a half-filled glass on the table, and suddenly Helena felt unsure about helping him. She wasn't normally like that but I guess the blood sort of chilled her guts. The man pulled himself into a sitting position and growled in pain. "Please give me the water or I'll die." The man said softly.

Helena said, "Look, I don't know your terms…I fear I might misjudge this situation and get into more trouble than I'm able to bear."

"I have been tied up here for days without a meal. My accusations on treason are tramped up. But look at stomach -" the man said, raising his shirt, revealing a gut sliced open. Shocked, Helena rushed and held the glass and took it to him. The man lifted his tied hands and took the glass and drank the water. Then he set

17

the glass down on the floor so that Helena bent down to pick it up, abruptly he grabbed the glass again and crashed the base into her head. Helena stumbled and fell on her back. The man had been tied hands and legs on plastic cords, so he started peeling them away, and was at last free. There was a window above him. He got to his feet and opened the bay window and climbed out. Now all he had to do was run as fast as he could. As he ran off, blood dripped from his shirt, and every stride drained his energy because he was running among thick bushes.

Sadly, the man had overestimated his chance at escape, failing to see that there were sentries on guard at the gate. But they traced him running off. So one of them drew an arrow and aimed at him and struck his shoulder, and the man fell headlong. They set out with their dogs to recover the man and found him trying to get back to his feet. "Hey, it looks like we've caught out a suspect, escaping from justice." One of the guards said with a notorious tone, to which the man cried back, "Please don't hurt me anymore."

The guard tossed him a dagger and it fell down at his feet. "I don't get the meaning of this." The man said, pointing at the dagger, and looking at them pitifully. The dogs barked nearly all at once. "Sir, freedom is a fortune to men," another guard said, "But it exists elsewhere except on the Earth, yet the good book says that blest are t' hands of a worker, and that destiny is got by chance, and not a choice." Shivering, the man said, "What do you want with me?" "Bless your hands, to save you," the guard said, and they at once released the three dogs, and the dogs ran up at the man while he bent down, jumped at him, knocked him down, and started to gnaw his body. The man first howled in bitter anguish, and then the cries slowly fell, and at last, he shut his eyes as he died quietly. The dogs ran back to the sentries, blood dripping from their mouths.

Back in the room in which Helena was detained, she started to stir awake and saw a faint shadow in the room. Scared, she sat up quickly, but there was no one! Then another shadow darted across the wall. Helena looked out and she saw a nearby tree, quietly she walked up to the window and opened the casement, and she saw a raven perched on a branch and staring down at her. Goodness, he was so old and looked so wise, Helena waved at him and he quickly rose on his wings and flew away.

Suddenly, the door was opened and two men came in, both held her by the arm, and dragged her out. Then they handcuffed her. Helena decided that she'd try as much as possible to be quiet since all her first efforts to speak for herself had only worsened things. Although the two men frightened her, she still wore her resolve not to show any sign of weakness. As the men dragged her back into the General's office, the General lowered his eyes to the papers, so he looked like he hadn't seen her, and the men dragged her out of his office.

There was a white car parked outside. Helena was forced into the backseat and the car was started and driven away. The King of Leno was very bio-conscious; for a long time he had been wary of the effects of pollution, and at last, he advised his council to criminalize the ownership of private cars, which were obviously polluting the environment. In exchange, he subsidized the prices of horses. Almost throughout the Kingdom horses were seen everywhere. The automobiles were only used by the government.

When Helena saw that the men were just as reluctant to speak as she was, she had a change of mind, "Excuse me, Sir," she said, and looked at the man beside her, "Where are you taking me?"

The driver took the question instead, "To the King's court!"

Helena opened her mouth to say more, but the driver looked in the rearview mirror, and warned her, "Lady, don't disturb the peace of our car, and if you say one word more…by heaven, I'll stuff you into a sack and smack you like a snake. So, keep your mouth shut like before!"

After the driver said that, the other man next to Helena robotically turned his head at her, lowered his gaze to her chest, reached his hand at her breasts and fondled them, Helena squeaked in protest. "Calm your tits, bitch." the man said and drew back his hand. Helena became quiet again. They were going at a mild speed because all government cars had been installed a speed governor. She thought of how she might break away from these men, and quietly tightened her fists, realizing how hard it was. When she thought on her situation well Helena saw she was lucky. She could well have fallen in the hands of beasts and got assaulted. Yet, as she knew it, she'd invited the harassment by her captors from speaking first.

Helena had nothing else on her mind but ways to escape. Since her wrists were tied together against her back, one method was to leap from her seat and crash through the window and fall on the road, but the action was much too grisly for a female hand. She actually shut her eyes visualizing the fall. Another method was to start on the men with death kicks and twin blows and take over the car. That was so much fun except it wasn't realistic. Like, if the man beside her gave her just one blow, she'd shit her pants. Another scenario showed her having superpowers to fling the men out, while they scream for pity, and she actually giggled at the thought.

"Marco?" The driver called, and the man beside Helena said, "The cunt seems too excited, perhaps at the imagination that she can suck on balls to get freedom. Watch her face."

It was around 6:07 in the evening. The driver looked in the rearview mirror, to check her face "Hahaha…"

All of a sudden, the car screeched out of the road, and Helena screamed in horror. The car rammed into a tree and the driver's blood splattered the windscreen. Nervously, Helena glanced about, and the man beside her had shut his eyes although he was still alive. There was a knife tucked in his belt. Helena turned her back and groped his waist and took the knife. The man opened his eyes, but he was too late because Helena had quickly stood, and plunged the knife into his chest, and stabbed him many times more until he released Helena and fell dead. Hastily, she went in front and searched out the key in the driver's pockets. Finally, she set herself free! Looking at her hands, they were red. Her heart was beating so quick that breathing nearly became labored. The car smelled like rotting metal. Helena wiped her hands on the man's trousers, unsuccessfully, and opened the door.

She was lost in grassland, but she wouldn't trace back her home. Helena also feared wild animals to pop out and give her a mess. In the distance, Helena saw two heads bobbing above the grass, and it occurred to her the men were galloping toward her. The next second, she saw a dark spot in the air, and the arrow zoomed in pretty fast and struck her shoulder, and she fell on her side. The men came up to her and dismounted. They were tall men, big men. One of them walked up to the car and opened the door. He cringed and crashed the door shut. The other man walked up to Helena, and pulled out the arrow, then lifted her onto his shoulder, and carried her to his horse. Helena drooled at her mouth. The two men mounted back their horses and one of them held a phone to his ear, "We found them. Only the girl survived." With that, they pulled on the reins and cantered away.

It was starting to get dark, and there was an enormous cloud in the sky. Suddenly, the door of the car was kicked open, and the driver stumbled out. He looked grisly! He stumbled to the rear window and peered in. His colleague (Marco) had lain dead with an open mouth. The man held his knees and cried in anguish. Then he stood up and turned around; not a long distance from him, he saw what looked like a pair of bright globes; prompting him to look keenly, O hell, it was a lion! He started to tremble, and the lion jogged toward him. Quickly, he smashed the side window of the car, reached his hand in, and grabbed a gun. The lion was about to open his mouth when he fired at him twice and he fell down. It started to get dark. And the man set off on foot, holding his gun, bowing his head.

Chapter 2

When Helena recovered consciousness, she was lying on the floor, and slowly, she opened her eyes and looked over the high ceilinged barn. Suddenly, there were footfalls coming in that direction. She rose to a sitting position, and her heartbeat quickened. As the door got opened, a circle of light leaked in, highlighting the dark floorboards. Two men walked in and crashed the door shut, blocking out the sunlight. The bigger man stayed at the door, while the other man came up to Helena, and when he stopped Helena's feet started trembling. The man had on a coat, with a hood many sizes too large, so it covered his face halfway.

"My delights are borderless, lady, for you're in my custody." The man growled with a deep voice. "But, we will not allow more time to pass, before handing you justice; I am also warned, lady, that your desire for autonomy is colossal."

"Who are you?" Helena cried.

A moment passed, and the man took a stride, pulled back his hood, exposing his shaven head. "Look up at me, lady." Slowly Helena lifted her eyes, and she saw the dark, mean, cold eyes staring back at her. Helena suddenly thought he wasn't human. She lowered her gaze at his hands, half expecting to see iron claws, and her attention was caught by a red flicker on his belt.

"So, now that both of us are no longer strangers, I shall with no more delay execute the order from my liege." The man grumbled again. "Lady, please be upstanding."

"Sir, tell me where I am," Helena said while standing up, and trying to balance her feet.

"We are in the royal grounds, lady," the man said, and then he added, "Opulence and gold lie beyond these walls. So, tell me how befitting is that?"

"It scares me."

"It is writ, a lady by the conduct of mind a man lives, and his action shall be weighed on the scales, to balance out the high standards of men. If this place scares you, it is not anyone else's fault but yourself." The man said and touched her head, "be steady, and ask no more."

Almost robotically, he turned away and walked back up to the big man still at the door. The two men had a quick word. And then there was a faint cling of metal. The man walked back up to Helena, with his hands folded in his back, but Helena got too wary of him, particularly since she'd made out the tiny cling, she tried to guess what he was holding; a dagger? Helena noticed something else; the man had put on shades, and the flicker on his belt had turned from red to green.

"Turn around, lady." The man said, and Helena suddenly thought he might kill her, so she faltered. The man held up the key, "I want to set your hands free, lady. Turn around." Helena turned around, and the man opened her handcuffs, setting her hands free. Then a moment passed, and suddenly dozens of spotlights were flicked on, hitting Helena's eyes with such a high intensity she got unconscious for a second. The light hurt her eyes so bad she screamed and rubbed her hands in her eyes. She screamed...screamed...screamed, and it looked like someone was turning up the light intensity with remote control. Helena fiercely rubbed her eyes, until blood ran out of them. Finally, she lay on the floor half dead.

The man lifted his finger, and the lights went out, he drew a torch-like sucking machine and walked up to Helena and knelt down beside her. A green light appeared on his shades, and he cradled the machine at Helena's left eye, sucking her eyeball out! He wrapped the eye in a white piece of paper with a star at the center. His partner joined him, and looked down at Helena, and said, "The boss seems to prefer a little boost nowadays."

"Yes," the man said, "I also like charged meals. They give me a reason to want to prolong my stay."

"The screams were wonderful." The man's partner said, "I'll also make her scream like that tomorrow...with my cock."

26

The man took off his shades and crossed his eyes and said, "I have never seen you with a woman."

"Is that an insult?"

"Hey, let's go."

They even decided to leave Helena's' hands free and walked out of the barn. Both men walked in step to their horses and mounted them and pulled on the reins. The horses neighed and cantered off. After a ten minute ride, they came around a bend and galloped along the wide road leading up to the palace. There were soldiers standing on every side of the road holding up shields. The King's court was a splendid work of architecture, with the walls supported by flying buttresses, and porticos held up by marble pillars. The palace stood out in an imposing regal way.

The two halted their horses, and the shades-man dismounted. His coattails billowing in the wind, he walked toward the emissary chambers and climbed down the stairs to an underground tunnel. Then he stepped on a gold hovercraft and closed his fists. Slowly, regally, the hovercraft ascended the high walled palace, lifting up the man, and the hovercraft stopped up near the royal stage. The King was at the throne, in a golden robe and a lustrous crown, his advanced age too prominent. He rose up and slowly came down the steps, his robe nearly sweeping the floor. There were two leopards at the base of the platform, resting on their paws, with sleepy eyes. The stage had a crescent periphery; but the King came up to the edge, placed his palm on the golden handrail, and gazed down at the man. The King radiated supreme authority, but the man bowed, and then looked back up.

"Ah, Daedo," the King said.

"Yes, my lord," Daedo answered, and held up the wrapped up cloth, "Your orders, my lord." The King put on a tiny smile at his mouth. He drew his hand from the handrail, and took a few steps sideward while looking down to Daedo still. The King's footfalls echoed back, gently. In a quick pace, the King said, "There's one notorious barrier that holds back a man from living out his dream. Would you take a guess, Daedo?"

Daedo shook his head up and down, and swallowed hard, "Fear; my lord, I think it cripples you."

"No." The King said and turned at him, "Lack of sight, Daedo," a minute of silence passed and the King sternly added, "I will always avenge my kindred's blood with more blood, not since unlike the ones before me I lack heart, but rather I deem man as undeserving to pity. Ah, my sweet son Daedo, today you please me and I need us to talk more." The King walked back up and sat in his throne and pulled on a lever. Swiftly, Daedo's hovercraft lifted and anchored at the royal stage, and a segment opened apart, so Daedo walked through the gap, and when he got in the stage, the segment closed up, magically.

Daedo looked up at the King and said, "Thanks for letting me in, my lord."

"I'm not your lord," the King said, smiling, standing up. "I'm your father. So, call me father."

"Father," Daedo said, "I have been always loyal to you, even though you barely reward me like the other children."

"All the great men in the world never do it for the penny," the King said, "They just do it to do it. Besides, you'll take over a part of the throne when I'm no more."

"Father, you excite me," Daedo said and looked away. Then he put on a smile and said, "Also, you bring up a very important thing."

"What's that?" The King said quickly. "I'm listening, spit it out, son."

"No, before we start, please take your parcel," Daedo said and held out his hand. The King suddenly took a dislike at his attitude, and with a hint of impatience, the King said, "Just feed them my cats."

"O, the leopards," Daedo said, calling them to mind, and turning around to look at them. Quietly, he walked up to the sleeping leopard and set down the eye in front of the leopard. As he walked away, Daedo heard a scraping noise at the floor, and he turned around to see the leopard munching away.

Daedo's words had brought the King curiosity, and when Daedo turned back, he saw the King fast coming down the steps. The King raised a finger, tackling him, "You were saying that I mentioned an important thing to you, what is that? Is it the throne?"

"Father –"

"Getting things from me is what you only care about? I'm ashamed!"

"I don't want anything from you!" Daedo defended himself. "I only want the truth."

"I don't get your meaning." The King said, furrowing his brow, and then wondered, "Did I tell any lies?"

"You hid a lot of things from me, father." Daedo said, "You always thought I'd believe you and just turn away."

The King asked, "Tell me what I hid from you?"

Daedo swallowed, and replied, "The truth about my mother, your rightful queen." Daedo cleared his throat, and said with a shaky little voice: "My mother is not dead."

Daedo's words stung the King so that the King was unable to move for a moment, and both remained silent, although Daedo quaked for rage, dying to swing a blow at his father's eye. But, soldiers were at the summit of the palace, stationed to look after the

King. If Daedo hurt the King the soldiers would obviously shoot arrows down to his back.

"You're a most thankless child," the King said, half trembling, and coughed on his fist, "May your perdition by heaven be my vengeance."

Daedo did not even hear well, and through clenched teeth, he said, "If she's really dead, father, let's dig out her remains, and examine what's left."

The King suddenly gave him a slap and breathed, "You have lost your mind, Daedo."

"If there's nothing to hide, you won't tackle me, right?"

The King's eyes burning red, he yelled, "Get out of my palace!" He took quick breaths. "Just get out of here and leave me alone!"

Daedo turned away and walked into the hovercraft. Then he turned back to his father. He put his hands in his pocket and held up an eight-inch platinum key, "Father, I have access to the royal tombs. I will dig out the truth."

With a weak voice, the King said, "If death the price be, I'm all for it, but I won't allow anyone dishonor my rested wife." the King coughed again, longer than before, "I warn you, Daedo, if you treasure life please don't follow on your plan."

"Threats, ah, what are you going to do kill me?" He asked with a sarcastic look, "All my life I slaved under you like an animal and you still held me in contempt."

"You're bitter for no reason."

"I don't want to pry eyes off men anymore."

"See, you're nasty, Daedo, was it much work to avenge your brother's death?"

"You don't treat me like you treat your children by other women, so I never cared for him anyway."

"Your disposition is erratic," the King said, "That's why I keep you in the shed. You just need to grow up, act like one of us, and I'll let you in."

"Wow, that's great," Daedo replied with sarcasm. The King walked back up and flipped a lever. Daedo stared at his feet as the hovercraft came back down onto a landing. He was in such a foul mood, blood vessels stood out on his face. He walked off and rushed down the stairs, walked in a lit tunnel, and came to the emissary chambers. He saw some errant folk getting disciplined with a whip, and they yelled fiercely at every lash. Daedo walked on to the main hall and opened the titanic doors just a little more than a crack, and he walked out. He looked over and saw Marco was still waiting for him, with a small frown. Marco's the guy with a hard-to-crack face, almost at all times, he had a blank look. Very few things ever made him excited. Daedo walked up and mounted his horse. He'd stayed longer than he promised not to and Daedo felt responsible to give an apology. "Marco, my old man gave me hell today, that's I overstayed."

"Save that, asshole," Marco replied, with a small laugh, exposing even smaller teeth.

"Asshole…you like saying that a lot," Daedo teased him. "Or I'm reading more into a casual insult than it's sensible?"

With an odorless, tight voice, Marco said, "You're too aware of that word, maybe that's the bigger issue."

"I don't get what you mean, Marco."

"Go and take a shitter."

Daedo curled his lips, "Not funny." They were still sitting on their horse's side by side. Marco's ears picked up a whizzing sound, and he turned around. Suddenly, an arrow pierced Daedo's back, and his upper body came down onto his thigh, wounded. A curtain was drawn across at the palace. Quickly, Marco grabbed Daedo by the armpits and heaved him into his horse, so that Daedo lay face down across the horse's back. Marco pulled the arrow off Daedo's back and tossed it down. Then he pulled on the reins and cantered off. As he was left behind, Daedo's horse growled and shuffled, looking anxious. The whole scenario had happened so quickly only a few guards took notice. Marco rode the horse to the servant quarters, where Marco lived, a distance of three kilometers from the palace. He had worried that the attacker might track down Daedo if he'd taken him back into his house at the royal court. He helped him walk in the house and he dressed his wound. Three hours later, night fell. Daedo claimed that his back wasn't hurting too bad but when he slept he even turned on his back without a problem.

At early morning the next day, Daedo woke up before Marco, and he walked out of the house. Marco's horse was lying in the stable. He went back in and put on a shirt. Daedo had awoken feeling totally differently today as if he had suddenly changed. He thought on how he'd dig out the truth about his mother. Although he knew that the King was behind the arrow, he also knew that if he went under, guards would be sent to look for him. Suddenly, Daedo realized he'd hit back by taking away something from him! Inspired by the thought, he walked into the stable and shook the horse awake and led him out. Then he mounted and cantered off.

He rode the horse to the detention chambers and dismounted. Carefully, he studied the guards from a distance, wondering whether they had been notified to arrest him, and he was torn between taking an open chance and breaking in. Although the guards knew Daedo well, their allegiance was to the King, so he had good reasons to be afraid. At last, he braved up and walked in through the gates. His heart was pounding when he was let in. He quickly walked up toward the last segment, where the girl killer had been confined, opened the doors, and walked in.

The girl was still awake, frightened, "Who is it?"

"Someone you need."

"Please don't hurt me," the girl said and whimpered.

Quietly Daedo came up to the girl and said, "Get your ass up." The girl still hesitated, so Daedo held her by the arm, and lifted her up. She groaned and said, "What do you want from me?"

"Get you out of this place."

"I don't trust you."

"I don't need that." The detention camp had been built adjoining a barn. Daedo crashed open the next door and they entered the barn. He was grabbing Helena and for crazy reasons, she had become very still. The barn was filled with all sorts of farm materials and at the middle was a tunnel, by which materials from the main depot would be belted around. The technology made it so much easier to distribute things than to carry things around mechanically. Carefully, Daedo instructed Helena to lower herself into the tunnel, and he got in after her. He knew much of the tunnel network, so he led her pretty well out of the chambers zone, and when they came to an open ground, they decided to take a chance. At this point, success was just about them if they'd crack the last step.

Daedo swallowed hard and informed Helena they'd now climb out of the tunnel; she had decided to trust him. As Helena felt the steps with her feet, Daedo held her waist, steadying her, climbing up after her. Helena came out and sat beside the hole. Daedo anchored his hands firmly at the edge and pulled himself out. The moonlight gave the area a gleam. They had managed to get out of the camp unnoticed. But the horse was standing a bit far.

"Helena, stay here for a minute, while I go and bring back the horse."

"Please don't leave me alone." Helena moaned and snuggled around his waist, "I'm terrified."

"Let's go then," Daedo said, and they started walking, carefully, and both were too alert to watch for any problems arising. The horse was a bit far but still, they kept at it. Finally, they came to the horse and mounted, and under the moonlight, they cantered away.

In the morning, just like Daedo had predicted, the King sent for him, but since he wasn't at his house, the King ordered his arrest. Immediately, Daedo became a wanted man.

Daedo fled to the town nearest the royal courts, where everyone owned a horse, and it was so easy to blend. In that town, not many people would have known who he was. While one might recall having seen that face in the palace, one wouldn't have known he was actually a royal son, since Daedo had not been created to show off. So, as the two went about the town looking for a place to stay, they were too carefree.

When the King learned that the girl killer was also missing, he linked it to Daedo and made stronger his resolve to capture him. He put a reward against his head. The King wanted him desperately because of the platinum key he had shown him, but he also wanted him for aiding the escape of the girl. So, troops were sent away to track him down.

Suddenly, Daedo spotted a group of horsemen in the town, and it startled him. He spun the horse and headed for another direction. After a short time, he turned around anxiously, and he noticed the men had picked him out of the crowd and were following him. One of the men drew a bow and shot out an arrow. Since Daedo was riding the horse from behind Helena, the arrow got him at the back, again. Helena watched in horror as Daedo fell off the horse. The men came and stopped around the fallen man. They were all dressed in cloaks and boots. They bound together Daedo's arms and lifted him onto the horse.

After a short time, the horse slowed down and stopped, somewhat agitated. Helena didn't know how to pull on the reins and make the horse move again.

So, she decided to dismount and go by foot for the rest of her journey. Besides, riding a horse would make her too observable, which was simply asking for more than she was ready to bear. On foot, it was easier to blend and take the narrow footpaths and walk in the alleys, without a lot of people noticing you. But what surprised Helena was the lack of remorse at losing Daedo. She might say that Daedo deserved a sip from the cup of agony, just like many others endured under his father's tyranny. For whatever reason, she wasn't too unhappy about losing him to the beast folk, a man who had in all senses helped her escape.

Helena walked down a path, and she came to a bend, and she was split between turning around and walking straight on. Then someone tapped her shoulder, startling her. "You were with that man that fell off the horse, right?" Helena swallowed hard, thinking that she had been caught up to as well, and she was prepared to deny him, but the stranger removed his hand from his pocket and held up a key. "When he fell off, this jumped out of his trousers." Helena peered at the key. "He told me to give you this key."

"Were you looking for me? You have tracked me down?" Helena wondered, thinking that his story wasn't adding up. "This key will open his mother's tomb…" and before he finished off, suddenly a name was called and the stranger looked away, replying, "Trying to see." Helena looked up and saw a cloaked man! Good golly! Was she being set up? Swiftly, she kicked the man's balls, and he groaned and crumbled. Helena snatched the key from him and turned away and ran off. Glancing back, the cloaked man started after her quickly, and then he lifted a bow. Thankfully, Helena saw a gap along the path and dodged around, giving her an open chance. She ran and ran until she was out of breath, and when she turned back, she had lost her enemies.

But that wasn't enough to make her feel at ease. As long as she was out on the street, she was still exposed, and still vulnerable. When she walked a few paces down she saw a string of rest houses built for travelers and foreign individuals. At this rate, it seemed to her the gods were on her side. She walked up to the entrance and she was stopped and asked to produce her ID, which she didn't have. However, after a long discussion, she was finally given a key and let in. She went into her room and sat in a couch and thought hard on whether it was time yet to travel back home. Then she took out the key and examined it. The key was too long and slim and polished, but then she pondered over the stranger's claim that the key would open Daedo's mother's tomb. Was that true? But she was supposed to care? Helena was tired of caring about things all her life.

When the hooded men seized Daedo, they tied him up, loaded him atop a horse, and rode back to the royal court with him. The King had ordered that he first be brought to him. On the way there it was so uncomfortable riding at his position, and he complained, and the men answered by choking his mouth. When they got to the palace, he was carried away into an underground room, where he was made to sit on a chair, and the oppressor jerked up Daedo's head and gave him a jug of water. Then the other men stood back a few paces. The King stepped forward, eyes still burning, and a rush of disappointment poured in Daedo's heart.

The King glared at Daedo's oppressor, warning him to step back, and Daedo's head dropped to his chest.

Steadily, the King walked toward him, and said, "You cannot escape from me, son."

"I'm not your son!" Daedo blurted and looked at him with rolled-up eyes.

The King waved him aside, and said, "To the point of this meeting. Let's make a deal. Hand me the key and you'll walk out a free man."

Slowly, Daedo looked at the King in his eyes. The King had a civil expression. Daedo said, "I gave them the girl."

Although he still looked calm, a blood vessel stood out on the King's face. He walked up to his men and closed in on their commander. "Where's the girl?"

"She slipped, my lord, by accident"

"I want the key, damn it!" The King fumed.

"Our men are still trying to track her down."

"I want her killed!" The King said.

"Killing her is not the problem," the commander said, "Finding her." Distressed, the King turned away, and then he said, "Beat him up and then let him free."

"Yes, my lord."

As soon as the King got out, the men jumped at Daedo with kicks and blows, and he screamed and called on his father. Then at last, just as they had been ordered, they asked him to leave. Daedo stumbled out of the room and held onto a pillar. A military cousin saw him all bloodied and he gave a hand and carried him back into his house. For weeks, he led a solitary life, avoiding any contact with the world. At this time he was struggling to find the answer to his problems. Ever since he was young his family had never taken him seriously. At this point, he was ready to open his eyes and see the truth, or better, disprove the lie. He had settled on turning against his father's wish.

One morning he walked into his private room and opened the cabinet. There was a safe in there. Daedo took hold of it and fiddled with the codes, and suddenly the lock yielded. He smiled and looked at the other twin golden key lying on soft cotton. Both the golden key and platinum key worked as a unit since most of the royal equipment were opened doubly. The keys, which Daedo had got from his mother, opened not only the royal graves but also any

41

item ever locked by a key since one could adjust the mouth and shaft to any size. But the golden key particularly had magical abilities. It seemed to radiate a deep frequency, with a delicate effect on one's level of mental plane, so that everything suddenly felt almost spiritually charged rather than physical. It was an odd experience.

The effects of Daedo's beating gradually had fallen. So he was ready to be the brave man and look on to what had got down years ago. He crowded his belongings into a bag and walked out and mounted his horse and cantered away. He would go to the town to relax before he took on his mission. Along the journey, he learned how the golden key raised his vibrations so that he'd tap what felt like revelations. Suddenly, life was not a mystery anymore. He had a renewed inexplicable spiritual energy about him that decoded everything on his way. When he looked at things he saw them in their exact design and purpose and could even read minds and tell what was about to happen. It was strange, that feeling, for it first looked like a rush of arrogance, but gradually the warmth of his conviction came out. When he reached the town finally, Daedo rode toward the center, and he kept sensing a disturbance he might not explain yet. As if by magic, he seemed to have an image of the town already in his mind, but he was attracted to this side of the road, and he kept hanging around. It was such a hard to explain moment, but he felt it, and all he had was hope that something might come of it. To his shock, he saw Helena mixing with the crowd!

Quickly, Daedo dismounted and started to track her down. He couldn't just sneak behind her and tap her shoulder and surprise her. Daedo hadn't known exactly what Helena thought of him. She might well remember that he was the man that gave her nightmares. So what would make her think he had got different? On his side, Daedo hoped that she kept in mind he'd helped her escape from the hands of death, and the tortures he did on her were merely orders by the hierarchy, but not what he'd have civilly done. Although the critic on his mind was too harsh, he still hoped that Helena would give him a chance to hear him.

So, he kept on trailing her, watching her relentless backward glances, and wondering how she failed to see him. Obviously, she was too nervous. Then he saw where she was about to enter; the lodging facility built by his majesty! For one to be allowed in the gate, he first provided an ID. That wasn't a problem to Daedo, for he had a royal passport, but when the workers saw that they'd suddenly be nice to him. He watched as she got in, still nervous as if she doubted her freedom an accident. Then he went hard and held up his royal badge and was let in without a problem.

Helena was walking down the hallway when he called to her. She lifted her eyebrows and turned around. The next second, she spun away and raced down, and knocked open a door. Daedo ran up too and pushed his way past the door before she had locked him out.

Calmly, he looked around the house as Helena fumed, "Please go away!"

"Helena, please sit down and hear me out."

"I don't have time for that!" Helena seethed, adding, "But I don't recall ever telling you my name."

"If it wasn't for me you'd still be in the death house," Daedo said, pointing a finger at his chest, and trying to look special.

"But I'm not in the death house anymore," Helena said and walked a few steps. "I don't want more troubles in my life. Please turn back and go away, sir."

Casually, he said, "Life is trouble."

"How did you trace me?"

Daedo slowly walked up to her, and she moved back, suddenly too aware of him. Then he drew the golden key from his pocket and Helena peered at it. Surprised, Helena thought that the platinum key in her pocket looked just like this one, except the color. Daedo held up the key, "This, Helena, helped me trace you down."

She lifted her eyebrows. "I don't get you."

"You have the twin, right?" Daedo said, and put on a tiny smile at his mouth, "The platinum key."

"Sit down," Helena said and locked her door. Then she turned around, "Please tell me more."

Chapter 3

The King's men had been combing the town, looking for the girl, but wisely they figured she might be staying at the free house. They decided to go by and ask about her. The man they met at the gate was a little crazy. It was nearly impossible to keep a reasonable dialogue with him. Frustrated, the King's men lifted him and crashed his bones on the floor. He wailed and cursed and limped after the men, warning them off, but he took another blow to his head and broke his mouth. The King's men were egotistic and full of arrogance. They went around bashing doors and asking occupants to all come out. The noise caught the attention of both Daedo and Helena. Her heartbeat quickening, Helena rushed to the door, opened only a crack and peered out. The men were not far from their room. And the men had a register of all rooms occupied, so it wasn't that they went away if nobody had responded; instead, it raised suspicion.

Helena turned at Daedo, and said, "Do something for goodness sake."

"Are you worried about them finding us?" Daedo asked, with a sarcastic tone. "Well, I don't have to worry. I have paid my dues already."

"When I saw you I knew you had come with trouble! You're in league with them!" Helena accused him, wearing a deep frown. "What do you want from me?"

"One thing only, trust," Daedo said and rubbed his palms in his knees. Then the fuss outside stopped at their door and suddenly there was a bang, followed with, "Jane! Open the door! I give you five seconds, beyond that the door goes down!" Then the men pounded the door again. "Open up, Jane! Open up!"

After about ten seconds and nobody had opened yet, the men started pounding the door, and the door was budging under the blows. Daedo asked Helena to hand him the platinum key and she quickly gave it to him. Masterfully, he merged the keys together, but a soft bluish glow came out around the keys. Watchfully, Daedo put down the keys on the floor, and a beam shot upward at the ceiling and then broadened to form a cone outline. So, it looked like a big cone of blue light. The pounding at the door got relentless.

Daedo stretched his hand to Helena, and said, "Hold on to my hand." She was too stunned to move. He quickly held her by the hand and both walked in the blue cone glow. Suddenly, the whole package spiraled into a higher dimension. The door crashed open, and the King's men stomped in, but they looked stupid since nobody had been there. Proudly, they marched out to their next victim and started slamming the door and howling with rage. Around thirty minutes later, Daedo and Helena reappeared in the room, in a tight hugging position, and the beam fell down to the key and faded out. Helena rushed and closed the door. Although she hadn't known Daedo as a blessed hand, she still decided to like him. The sudden change in attitude was hard to believe since now she looked as if she couldn't bear life without him.

"What's next?" Helena asked, and stared, waiting for an answer.

"We've got to leave, Helena." He said and adjusted his throaty voice. "And go to Dibano by train."

"Where's that?" She asked with a frown.

"A coastal town North of Zegos, we could stay there tomorrow, and start on our final journey the next day."

"I have got to trust you." Helena said, "Although I don't even quite know you."

"My name is Daedo," he said and fought back a smile in vain. "But there is a clever way for strangers to know each other, don't you think?"

"Yah, I guess, telling stories," Helena said, and Daedo laughed a bit and walked up to her. He leaned down to her, "You don't get it…"

"Oh, now I do," she said and leaned in so that they kissed like lovers.

Suddenly, a man burst into the house and Daedo spun around. "Oh, it's them!" The man shouted, and as he turned away, Daedo jumped at him and fought him down. He was a big man beside Daedo, yet was dominated at last. For a whole minute, they pushed and struggled on the floor. When he got the chance, Daedo smacked his face, to the man's mournful cries. Finally, Daedo sat on the enemy's chest and whacked fists at his head and left him half dead. Suddenly, there were oncoming footfalls down the hallway! Daedo and Helena ran up to the casement and climbed out. They jumped down onto a littered alley and walked off to blend into the crowds.

At night, they got on a train for Dibano and arrived early morning the next day. In most part of the journey, Helena placed her head on Daedo's chest. At Dibano they acquired new items and spent the day exploring the coastal town; particularly admiring buildings against the seashore background. They held to one another as newlyweds on a holiday. At around four in the evening, they went out at sea to sail away in an island named Heloda; a hilly, forested, semi-anarchistic society. Heloda was still a protectorate of Leno, yet the monarchy had failed to look after it. So, her people organized themselves to form a nation. According to some heretics, the monarchy had been reluctant to develop Heloda on purpose, since they'd permitted an alien tribe to inhabit the forest. To an average Lenoan though, the theory was outrageous, and juvenile, for Lenoans believed that their lord neither would in anything insensitive take part nor do them harm. The rumor was spread by a few individuals, who were often rounded up, and bashed in public. For outcasts and misfits, Heloda was heaven, obviously because of the anarchical society. The island had a small population, but most of the land was covered with trees.

When their boat docked at the other end, Helena looked out at the town, and she thought it quite livable. The buildings weren't tall, but the antique designs looked well, and minarets at housetops seemed a trend here, except they were built from a hardwood. They climbed out and went into the town. The townsfolk were big on smoking, a first put off, Helena thought. The air of defiance hung heavy all over the town. The first thing they did was report to the governor so they'd be assigned a job and also a place to live. They wrote down their names and stated their plans there. But Daedo never gave out his royal identity for fear that he might be tracked down. The governor asked them to list their skills in order to evaluate their potential. Daedo wrote he was good at defense skills and handling weapon and riding horses. Helena said she was only good at keeping house and doing casual work. Normally, it took a few days before one came back to get a response on job placement, yet the governor suddenly posted them into a military station near the fringe of the forest.

Daedo didn't want any more attachment to the forces, and he was also curious about the governor's motivation, and he said to him, "Sir, we're quite foreign in this land, I mean to say, a military outpost is too much work for us… don't you think?"

The governor was wearing a robe and a breast coat. "Daedo and Helena, this is your first time to come here." He said with a sharp voice, looking up at them both, and Helena's heartbeat quickened, anticipating awful news. "I welcome you to the nation of Heloda. This is a place unlike any other you have been to. But in order to count as a guest, you must visit with us more than once." The governor paused and looked at a hologram with figures running through the screen. "My records indicate that it's your first time here."

 Helena and Daedo both nodded, agreeing.

"Technically, you're alien." The governor clarified and took a sip from a dark mug. "We don't know your agendas, but if you stay long enough, you may qualify to get citizenship."

"If we stay? For how long?"

The governor brushed aside the question. "Citizens have the right to tell us what they want." He turned to his device again and tapped at the screen. Two badges flipped out of a wall portal. "Pick up your badges and search out the house that matches your reference numbers."

Let's Stay Connected

Hey… this is Aurelia Hilton! Did you enjoy this book? I hope it was steamy & hot and you've absolutely enjoyed this short novel.

You know what? Let's stay connected! I will usually give out copies of my free short novels when I first release them to you, my lovely readers.

It is super simple to stay connected & updated with my future book releases…

Step 1: Join my email list:
http://bit.ly/aureliahiltonjoin

Step 2: Check out my other books! Simply google "Aurelia Hilton erotica books".

Once again, thanks for reading this short novel of mine & let's stay connected! **winks**

CPSIA information can be obtained
at www.ICGtesting.com
Printed in the USA
BVHW031109290819
557144BV00006B/79/P

9 781646 158119